BOY TROUBLE

by Diana G. Gallagher

illustrated by Brann Garvey

STONE ARCH BOOKS
www.stonearchbooks.com

Claudia Cristina Cortez is published by Stone Arch Books
151 Good Counsel Drive, P.O. Box 669
Mankato, Minnesota 56002
www.stonearchbooks.com

Library of Congress Cataloging-in-Publication Data
Gallagher, Diana G.
  Boy trouble / by Diana G. Gallagher ; illustrated by Brann Garvey.
    p. cm. — (Claudia Cristina Cortez)
  ISBN 978-1-4342-1576-5 (library binding)
  ISBN 978-1-4342-1757-8 (paperback)
  [1. Dating (Social customs)—Fiction. 2. Middle schools—Fiction. 3. Schools—
Fiction. 4. Hispanic Americans—Fiction.] I. Garvey, Brann, ill. II. Title.
  PZ7.G13543Bo 2010
  [Fic]—dc22
                                2009002559

Summary: Claudia has had a crush on Brad Turino for as long as she can
remember. She's thrilled when Brad asks her for help with homework. But
when cute new boy Rusty Alvarez moves to town and asks her out on her first
date, she doesn't know what to do.

Creative Director: Heather Kindseth
Graphic Designer: Carla Zetina-Yglesias

Photo Credits
Delaney Photography, cover

Printed in the United States of America

Table of Contents

Cast of

ME

CLAUDIA

That's me. I'm thirteen, and I'm in the seventh grade at Pine Tree Middle School. I live with my mom, my dad, and my brother, Jimmy. I have one cat, Ping-Ping. I like music, baseball, and hanging out with my friends.

MONICA is my very best friend. We met when we were really little, and we've been best friends ever since. I don't know what I'd do without her! Monica loves horses. In fact, when she grows up, she wants to be an Olympic rider!

MONICA

BECCA

BECCA is one of my closest friends. She lives next door to Monica. Becca is really, really smart. She gets good grades. She's also really good at art.

ADAM and I met when we were in third grade. Now that we're teenagers, we don't spend as much time together as we did when we were kids, but he's always there for me when I need him. (Plus, he's the only person who wants to talk about baseball with me!)

ADAM

Characters

TOMMY's our class clown. Sometimes he's really funny, but sometimes he is just annoying. Becca has a crush on him . . . but I'd never tell.

I think **PETER** is probably the smartest person I've ever met. Seriously. He's even smarter than our teachers! He's also one of my friends. Which is lucky, because sometimes he helps me with homework.

Every school has a bully, and **JENNY** is ours. She's the tallest person in our class, and the meanest, too. She always threatens to stomp people. No one's ever seen her stomp anyone, but that doesn't mean it hasn't happened!

ANNA is the most popular girl at our school. Everyone wants to be friends with her. I think that's weird, because Anna can be really, really mean. I mostly try to stay away from her.

Cast of

CARLY is Anna's best friend. She always tries to act exactly like Anna does. She even wears the exact same clothes. She's never really been mean to me, but she's never been nice to me either!

NICK is my annoying seven-year-old neighbor. I get stuck babysitting him a lot. He likes to make me miserable. (Okay, he's not that bad ALL of the time . . . just most of the time.)

BRAD has been my top-secret number-one crush for a really long time. He's the sports star of Pine Tree Middle School, a really nice guy, and super cute. I wish he was my boyfriend. Maybe someday . . .

Characters

RUSTY is a new kid at Pine Tree Middle School. He likes baseball, movies, and me!

RUSTY

GRANDMA

GRANDMA makes the best cinnamon toast in the world. I love it when she stays with us. I don't love talking to her about boy problems, but I have to admit she gives pretty good advice.

MRS. SANCHEZ is our English teacher. I love English, and she's one of my favorite teachers.

MRS. SANCHEZ

CHAPTER 1

ALL SHOOK UP

Today was my **lucky day**. I had lots of good luck and a little bad luck. It didn't quite even out. But more good luck didn't mean things would turn out great.

My dreams of **romantic bliss** could end in heartbreak.

Why?

Because I have a crazy mad secret crush on **Brad Turino**, gorgeous sports star and super nice guy.

Maybe I should start at the beginning.

The first good thing that happened today was that Mrs. Sanchez gave us the best English assignment ever. We have to write a six-page short story. I love to write. **It's like building with words.** I'm pretty good at it.

Then the news got better.

"The best stories will be *published* in the Pine Tree Middle School anthology," Mrs. Sanchez explained.

Anthology = collection of poems or stories

Writing a bestselling novel is on my *Exciting Things To Do When I Grow Up* list. Having a story in the school anthology was a fantastic place to start.

"**Imagination** and **style** will count as much as spelling and grammar," Mrs. Sanchez went on.

"Style?" **Carly** asked. She looked puzzled. "Do we get credit for what we *wear*?"

"No fair!" **Tommy** exclaimed. "Nobody can beat Anna and Carly in a **best-dressed writer** contest."

Anna Dunlap is the fashion expert and **number-one trendsetter** at our school. She's also popular, selfish, and **stuck up**.

She treats everyone like *DIRT*, but a lot of people idolize her. I don't get it.

Anna suddenly looked interested. "Do clothes really count?" she asked.

"No," Mrs. Sanchez said. "Writing style is how you use language to tell a story. It should be **entertaining and interesting**."

"Oh," Anna said. She went back to doodling in her notebook.

"What if you've never done anything **interesting** enough to write about?" **Adam** asked.

"A short story is fiction," Mrs. Sanchez said. "It's not true. The writer **makes up characters** and decides what happens to them."

Anna perked up again. "Can I write about a model that designs clothes and **gets rich** and becomes world-famous?" she asked.

Mrs. Sanchez nodded. "Yes, but make it **original**," she said. "Good stories put a new twist on old ideas."

My head was STUFFED with fantastic story ideas. That was the problem. I had to pick one. **But which one?**

After school, I walked home alone. Becca was at the dentist, and Monica's mom had taken her to the mall.

Then I heard *a boy's voice.*

"Claudia!" the boy called out. "Wait up!"

I stopped, looked back, and froze. **Brad Turino** was running toward me. I had a major uh-oh moment. Why was Brad Turino calling my name?

1. Were things dropping out of a hole in my backpack?

2. Did I have a "Chase Claudia" sign on my back?

3. Was I dragging toilet paper?

When Brad caught up, I just stared at him. My mouth hung open, and my eyes bugged out. My heart pounded, and my stomach **flip—flopped**. It was hard to breathe.

"I need a huge favor," Brad said.

"From me?" I squeaked.

"I have to get a good grade in English," Brad said, "or my dad won't let me play sports. Will you **help me** with my story?"

I opened my mouth, but nothing came out.

"Please," Brad begged. "You're the best writer in our class."

I nodded and mumbled, "Okay."

After Brad left, I raced home. I burst through the front door. I almost knocked Grandma Cortez off her feet. She was staying at our house while hers was being painted.

"Sorry, Grandma!" I cried. "Are you OKAY?"

"I'm fine," Grandma said. "How are you?"

"Flabbergasted!" I exclaimed. That's what Grandma says when something incredible happens to her.

"Good flabbergasted or bad?" Grandma asked.

"Good, I think, or maybe bad. It all depends," I said in a rush. I don't normally talk to my grandma about boy stuff, but I had to tell someone. "Brad is the cutest coolest guy in my class and he asked me for help but I can't help if I can't talk and he'll never like me if I let him down so I'll just have to try and hope he gets an A and doesn't think I'm a brainless dork," I told her.

"Oh, my," Grandma said. "No wonder you're in a tizzy."

Extreme tizzy was more like it! I babble when I'm frantic. And I can't sit still. I ran upstairs, dialed Monica's number, and left a message.

"You and Becca have to come over right away!" I said. "It's an emergency."

I hung up. Then I realized that my message might make Monica worry, so I called her back. "This is Claudia again," I said. "It's not a real-life emergency. It's a **love-life emergency!**"

I waited in the tree house until Monica and Becca arrived. Then I blurted out my story in another sentence that didn't pause for **punctuation**.

I was out of breath when I reached the period at the end of the sentence.

"That is so ₵ⵙⵙⳑ!" **Becca** exclaimed.

"It is?" I asked.

"Duh!" **Monica** said, rolling her eyes. "You've had a **crush on Brad** for years!"

"He asked you for help! This is **an amazing opportunity**!" Becca said.

Monica nodded. "You're Brad's **editor** now. That's a really great excuse to sit with him at lunch," she told me.

"Or call him," Becca added. "Brad might even start to like you back!"

"Not if I can't talk to him," I said. I sighed with frustration. "Who wants a *tongue-tied true love*?"

"Some boys like girls who don't talk," Becca said.

"That would be boring," I said. "Brad isn't boring."

"And maybe he isn't your true love," Monica said.

I gasped. "What do you mean?" I asked.

Monica shrugged. "Maybe you can't talk to Brad because deep down you know he's not your true love," she said.

"But I feel **warm and gooey** inside when I'm with him," I protested.

"I get chills when I'm near Tommy," Becca said.

"I don't have anyone like that," Monica said. "I guess I just haven't met the right one yet."

Monica had never had a crush, so she wasn't a **romance expert.** But her words still bothered me.

I've liked Brad a long time.

What if it was just a HABIT?

What if I didn't like him as much as I thought?

CHAPTER 2

CHANCE MEETINGS

Brad called that night after dinner. I was so nervous I almost SQUEALED into the phone.

I clamped my mouth shut. The squeal turned into a gurgled grunt. Then I got a **frog** in my throat.

"Hi, Brad," I said. It sounded like I was chewing gravel.

Brad didn't notice. (Or he was too nice to say anything.) He wanted my e-mail address. "Can I send my story now?" he asked.

"Sure! I'll read it tonight," I said. Then I realized something. I didn't choke up as much when I talked to Brad on the phone. **That was great!**

"Awesome," Brad said. "We can talk about it at lunch tomorrow."

I had a lunch date with Brad!

That was more good luck, right?

I *wish!*

I went to the computer and read Brad's story.

Brad's story was called "Madhouse." That was a great title for his action-adventure plot. But the writing was awful. The story was BORING and full of mistakes.

I knew how to fix it.

That was the problem.

Some boys don't like girls who are smarter than they are. That kind of boy really doesn't like girls who let them know it. Not even when they ask for help.

Was Brad like that?

I worried about it on my way to school the next day. I stared at my feet as I walked. I didn't see the boy on the sidewalk ahead of me. I plowed right into him.

"Ooof!" yelled the boy. He stumbled, but he didn't fall.

"Oh, gosh!" I said, wincing. "My fault. I wasn't watching where I was going."

"No problem," the boy said. "I was blocking
the sidewalk." He was **cute**, with brown eyes,
brown hair, and a friendly smile. I had never
seen him before.

"Are you new?" I asked.

"**Rusty Alvarez**," he said, "seventh grade
movie fanatic and **roller blade racer**." He
shook my hand. "We moved in last week."

"I love movies and roller blades!" I exclaimed.

Rusty grinned. "Then this is my LUCKY day," he
said.

I blushed. Rusty was **flirting** with me! "Claudia
Cortez," I said, "seventh grade baseball fan, odd
jobs entrepreneur, and cat lover."

"Do you go to Harmon County Hawks games?"
Rusty asked.

"Whenever I can," I said. "Are you going to Pine
Tree Middle School?"

Rusty nodded. He looked at the paper in his hand.
"My schedule says I have **homeroom** with Ms. Stark,"
he told me.

"Then this **really is** your lucky day," I said. "I'm in Ms. Stark's homeroom. Follow me."

We compared schedules as we walked to homeroom. Rusty was in most of my classes. He seemed like a **nice guy.** Not as nice as Brad, but pretty nice.

"So, what are the people like here?" Rusty asked.

"My friends are **pretty cool**," I said.

I gave Rusty a quick rundown on everyone. I didn't tell him about Anna the bossy snob and mean Jenny Pinski, our school bully. I didn't want to ruin his *first impression* of our school.

And I didn't give away anyone's secrets. But soon Rusty knew one secret — that **Tommy liked Becca.** We caught them holding hands by the bike rack. **AWKWARD!**

"Hi, guys!" I said.

Becca and Tommy dropped hands and turned red. **Becca** gave us a fake explanation. "I, uh — fell down," she said. "Tommy **helped** me up."

"Right," Tommy said. He nodded like a bobblehead. "I saved Becca from the **big, bad bicycles**."

I pretended to believe him. So did Rusty.

Then Anna and Carly walked over. They can't resist good gossip. If something interesting happens, they know about it first. Then they make sure everyone else knows about it, too.

Anna Dunlap Tells The World!

Anna's Story: *Super smart Peter Wiggins flunked a math test!*

The Real Explanation: *His new glasses were wrong, and he couldn't see.*

Anna's Story: *Sylvia plays with dolls!*

The Real Explanation: *She collects dolls. That's not the same thing!*

Anna's Story: *Larry Kyle swallows live goldfish whole!*

The Real Explanation: *He eats gummy goldfish, and he chews.*

Anna looked at Becca, then Tommy.

"What's going on?" Anna asked.

"We weren't **holding hands**," **Tommy** said.

Becca jabbed him with her elbow.

But Anna lost interest in Becca and Tommy when she noticed Rusty.

"Who are you?" Anna asked.

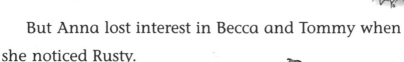

Rusty introduced himself.

Then I introduced everyone else. "Rusty, this is Becca, Tommy, Anna, and Carly," I told him.

"Nice to meet you," Rusty said. "**We should go,** Claudia. I don't want to be late on my first day."

Anna smiled sweetly. "I can show you around school, Rusty," she said.

I could tell that she thought he was CUTE.

"No, thanks," Rusty said. "I already asked Claudia to be my guide."

Anna's fake smile faded.

I was **astonished** and **pleased**.

The cute new guy had picked me over Anna Dunlap, the most popular girl in school.

THREE'S A CROWD

I had **serious jitters** when I walked into the cafeteria. Lunch with Brad was a 9.0 on my romance meter. Only two things ranked higher:

A real date with Brad = 9.5
Being Brad's girlfriend = 10.0

Brad was sitting at an empty table. I ducked into the food line before he saw me. I needed more time to plan.

I knew what to tell Brad about his story. I just didn't want to hurt his feelings or sound like a know—it—all.

Anna and Carly were a few kids ahead of me. They took their trays and walked toward Brad.

My heart sank. I can barely get my words out when I'm alone with Brad. I knew I'd stammer like a *hungry woodpecker* in front of Anna.

Then she'd use it to EMBARRASS me later. She's embarrassed me before.

1. Anna sent a mushy Valentine to loud, obnoxious Kevin Burns signed *"oooo & xxxx Love, Claudia."* He followed me everywhere for a week!

2. Last year Anna took a picture of me sitting on Santa's knee. Nick, the kid I babysit, wouldn't talk to Santa alone. The **school newspaper** printed the picture on page 1.

3. Anna told me and my friends that our school was having a **Stripes, Polka-dots, and Clashing Colors** day. We wore awful, mismatched outfits. Then Anna made fun of us.

But Anna wouldn't get me this time.

I watched as Brad said something to Carly and Anna. Then he waved at me. "Over here, Claudia!" he said.

Anna glared at me, but only for a second. She's too COOL to let a boy know she likes him. I'm too chicken.

I sat down across from Brad. I was too nervous to talk.

I gave him a goofy grin and fumbled my silverware.

"So, is my story any good?" Brad asked.

I chose my words carefully. "Well, uh — the plot is . . . very EXCITING," I told him.

That was honest. In Brad's story, two boys find a treasure map in the attic. The house changes into all the strange places on the map. That's why Brad's title is "Madhouse." The only way out is to follow the clues and find the treasure.

"Cool," Brad said. He grinned. "I thought it might be boring."

"It could be a little more thrilling," I said.

"How?" Brad asked. He wasn't upset. He was interested.

I took Brad's story out of my backpack. I read the first paragraph aloud.

John and Jerry didn't have anything to do. They went up to the attic to look around. Jerry found a rolled-up paper. It was a treasure map.

Brad frowned. "That sounds kind of lame," he admitted.

"But it's easy to fix," I said. "Picture what happens. Then write down what you see."

"I thought I did," Brad said.

I had to risk making Brad mad. It was the only way to help him.

"**Details** make stories more interesting," I explained. I took a deep breath. Then I rewrote his story out loud.

It was raining. John and Jerry were stuck inside. They were bored with video games and TV.

"Let's explore the attic," John said.

John and Jerry ran up the stairs. The attic was dark and gloomy. They opened an old chest. The hinges creaked.

"Then what happens?" Brad asked.

"It's your story," I said. "You tell me."

"Oh, I get it!" Brad said.

Then he continued rewriting the story out loud.

There was a rolled-up paper in the chest. It was yellow and torn.

"What's that?" Jerry asked.

John unrolled the paper. It was covered with lines and pictures. "It's a treasure map!"

"Perfect!" I said. I held two thumbs up.

Brad began to write in his notebook. He looked up and told me, "I want to write that down before I forget."

Just then, I saw Rusty leave the lunch line. He paused to look around.

"Over here, Rusty!" Anna called out.

I sighed. Anna had tried to pass Rusty a note in fourth period. **He ignored her.** I guess he didn't want to get in trouble his first day.

"We saved you a seat, Rusty," Anna called again.

Rusty ignored her again. He **smiled** when he saw me and hurried over. "Can I sit here?" he asked.

I didn't know what to say. I looked at Brad. He looked at Rusty and then back at me.

I didn't know what to do.

I had waited *my whole life* to have lunch with Brad Turino. Everything was going a zillion times better than I hoped. I wasn't even terribly tongue-tied!

I never dreamed a second cute boy would want to sit with me. Or that **two cute boys** would pick me over Anna!

Anna never thought two gorgeous guys would jilt her for me either. She was really furious. I could almost see **cartoon smoke** shooting out of her ears and nose!

I knew Anna was already plotting a way to get even. I didn't want to think about that. I wanted to be alone with Brad. But I couldn't say no to Rusty.

1. It would be rude.

2. It was Rusty's first day at school.

3. It was making Anna nuts.

"Sure. Have a seat," I said.

Rusty sat down beside me. I introduced him to Brad. "This is Brad Turino. I'm helping him with his story for English," I told Rusty.

"Hi, Rusty," Brad said, smiling. He stuffed his notebook and pen into his backpack. *"Do you like sports?"* he asked.

"I love sports," Rusty said. "Baseball is my favorite. I played third base at my old school."

"Cool!" Brad said. Then he stood up. "I have to go see Coach Johnson. See you later, guys!"

Then Brad left. **I wanted to cry**, and I never cry. Well, almost never.

I get WEEPY when my cat Ping-ping disappears. She always comes back, but not until I've imagined nine horrible feline fates.

Sometimes I **tear up** when Nick kicks me in the shins. He packs a lot of power for a little kid.

But nothing has ever made me **blubber or bawl** in public.

Not even being **CRUSHED** by the love of my life.

Brad left me alone with another boy.

It didn't bother him at all.

That proved it. He liked me as a friend, but he didn't like me **as a girl.**

"Brad seems like a good guy," Rusty said.

"He is," I said.

Brad was a great guy.

Until today. I smiled at Rusty. It wasn't Rusty's fault Brad had just broken my heart.

"What kind of movies do you like, Claudia?" Rusty asked.

"All kinds," I said. "I like science fiction and action-adventure the best."

Rusty looked surprised. "**Really**?" he asked.

"Why would I lie?" I replied.

"Most girls like sappy chick flicks," Rusty said. "I guess you're not like other girls." He put his hands over his heart, batted his eyes, and **faked a sigh**.

I GIGGLED. It was funny.

"I like chick flicks, too," I said. "I just like sci-fi and action movies better."

Then something amazing happened.

"Do you want to go see *Alien Hunter* with me?" Rusty asked.

CHAPTER 4

IT'S A DATE

I was so busy **talking to boys** I didn't finish my lunch. I was starving when I got home. Grandma made me a grilled cheese sandwich.

"Here's some milk to wash it down," Grandma said, handing me the glass. "How was school?"

Words zipped through my mind like flash cards: **fantastic**, weird, sad, shocking. I settled for something blah. I did not want to discuss my love life with Grandma.

"It was OKAY," I said.

"You were so happy this morning," Grandma said. She looked puzzled. "I thought today was **special**."

"No," I said. I shook my head. "Nothing special."

Grandma smiled and patted my hand. "I'm here when you're ready to talk about it," she told me.

I just nodded. Grandma knows when something's bothering me. **But she isn't pushy.**

FYI: Mothers and grandmothers know stuff because they felt the same way and did the same things when they were kids.

"Here's a snack for your friends," Grandma said. She gave me a paper plate. It was piled with warm chocolate chip cookies.

"Thanks!" I said. I ran outside with the cookies and my keepsake shoebox.

Monica and Becca met me in the tree house. We were going to work on our scrapbooks. We had been saving **Middle School Memories & Mementos.**

We ate cookies and sorted our supplies.

I did not want to talk about Brad. But of course, Becca and Monica didn't want to talk about anything else.

"You had lunch with Brad. And you didn't tell us!" Monica said, pretending to be annoyed.

"Did you save something for your scrapbook?" Becca asked.

"Like what?" I asked. **"His straw wrapper?"**

"Or **the napkin his lips touched**," Becca suggested. She giggled.

Monica rolled her eyes. "Just tell us what happened."

"Brad wanted to talk about his story," I said. "So we did. What are you putting in your scrapbook, Monica?" **I wanted to change the subject.**

"The poster from my first horse show," Monica said. She had won fourth place in a walk-trot-canter class last Saturday. Her white ribbon was hanging on her bedroom wall.

"Brad couldn't take his eyes off you at lunch," Becca said.

"Did he get 𝕁𝔼𝔸𝕃𝕆𝕌𝕊 when Rusty sat down?" Monica asked. "Is that why he left?"

"No," I answered honestly. "He had to go see Coach."

"What did you and Rusty talk about?" Becca asked.

That was too **big** to keep secret. I tried to sound **casual**.

"He asked me to go see
Alien Hunter," I told them.

Monica gasped. "Like on a **date**?" she asked.

"Oh my gosh, Claudia! That is so cool!" Becca
squealed.

"Your first date!" Monica exclaimed.

"I wish Tommy would ask me out," Becca said.
"Going in a group doesn't count."

Becca had a point. We went to the movies with
Peter, Adam, and Tommy all the time. **That wasn't the
same as a date.**

"I want to go see *Alien Hunter*!" Nick said. He stuck
his head in the door.

"What are you doing here?" I asked.

"I smelled COOKIES," Nick said.

"You can have a cookie," Monica said. She passed
the plate to Nick. "But you can't go to the movies with
Claudia."

"No fair!" Nick whined. "*Alien Hunter* is my
favorite movie!"

"It can't be your favorite," Becca said. "You haven't even seen it yet."

"That's why I want to go," Nick explained. He glared at me. Then he shrieked. **"I want to go! I want to go! I want to go!"**

Three weeks ago I wouldn't help Nick dig up worms, so he put glue in my shampoo bottle. I had to keep him happy. Otherwise I'd have to check my shoes for stones, thorns, and beetles every day.

How To Bribe Nick

1. Give in on your terms.

"Okay, I'll take you to see Alien Hunter on Sunday."

2. Be ready for Nick's argument.

"I want to go on Saturday!"

3. And make a better offer.

"I'll buy popcorn and soda if we go Sunday."

Nick took the deal, and I didn't have to take him on my date.

Suddenly, getting ditched by Brad didn't seem so **tragic**. Rusty Alvarez, roller blade racer, baseball player, and good-looking new guy, liked me.

As a girl.

CHAPTER 5

BAD TIMING

The **I'm-so-happy-Rusty-likes-me** balloon popped the next morning.

Did I really want to go to the movies with him? I didn't know. After all, I'd spent years imagining my first date with Brad.

Claudia's Dream Date with Brad

1. On the beach, at a carnival, or to the movies.

2. No parents, no friends, no Nick.

3. I don't stutter, hiccup, or burp.

I wasn't Brad's girlfriend, but I've like-liked him for a long time. Going out with someone else felt like cheating.

Should I call off my date with Rusty or keep it? I was still trying to decide when I walked into homeroom.

"Hi, Claudia!" Rusty said. He stood by my desk. He was talking to my friends.

"Guess what?" Adam asked when I slid into my seat.

Becca jabbed Adam.

Adam stopped talking.

Tommy didn't. "We all want to see *Alien Hunter*," Tommy said. "So let's go **together** next Saturday."

"Works for me," Peter said.

"I'm in," Adam said.

Becca and Monica looked at me. They thought the boys were *wrecking* my date. WRONG!

"It's okay with me," I said.

"It is?" Monica asked.

"Everybody's going anyway," I said.

"Good point," Becca agreed.

But it wasn't my only reason.

Three Reasons It Was Better to See Alien Hunter In A Group

1. It wouldn't be a real date.

2. I wouldn't be cheating on Brad by being on a date with someone else.

3. I'd still get to see the movie.

"Will your mom drive us, Claudia?" Rusty asked. "My parents are still unpacking."

"You and Claudia can ride with me, Rusty," Tommy said.

"Thanks," Rusty said.

"Hey, you can ride with us too, Becca," Tommy added.

"You and me with Rusty and Claudia?" **Becca** said. Her eyes got wide. They sparkled when she grinned. "I mean, okay. Sure."

Tommy hadn't exactly asked her out. But I know how Becca thinks.

Fact #1. Rusty and I were going on a date.

+

Fact #2. Becca and Tommy were riding in the same car.

=

Becca could pretend it was a double date.

I heard someone giggle. Then someone else whispered. I looked around. Anna smirked and looked away.

Were they talking about **Rusty and me?**

Brad rushed into the room, but he didn't stop at his desk. He headed **straight** for me.

My throat closed up. What did Brad want? Did he know I was going out with Rusty? **He didn't care, did he?**

The bell rang. Brad turned around and went to his seat. What did he want?

I didn't have to wait long to find out. He caught me in the hall before first period.

"Can you come to my house on Saturday?" Brad asked.

"Your house?" I repeated. My mind reeled. I felt dizzy. I squawked like a **parrot**. "This Saturday?"

"So you can read my story again," Brad explained. "Then we could watch a DVD or play pool, if you want."

If I want? **Was he kidding?** I'd give up soda and candy for a year to watch a DVD with Brad.

But as my uncle Diego always says, "Life isn't fair."

"I'm sorry, Brad," I said. "I can't."

Alarms clanged in my head. My inner voice screamed.

Are you nuts?

Brad Turino asked you over to his house.

Blond, blue eyes, great smile Brad!

And you said no! No!

How could you say no?

I didn't have a choice.

Everyone knew I was going to the movie with Rusty. Backing out now would be AWFUL.

Plus Becca needed me to make her date with Tommy seem real.

Anyway, it wasn't like Brad asked me out. **He didn't like-like me. He just needed a good grade in English.**

CHAPTER 6

RUMOR RIOT

I didn't want to talk about turning down Brad's invitation. But I couldn't hide **important** things from my best friends.

The questions started at lunch.

"Are you 𝕊𝕀ℂ𝕂 to your stomach?" **Becca** asked.

I wiped the grimace off my face.  "No, I'm fine."

"You don't **look fine**," **Monica** said.

I didn't dare speak. The truth was crouched on the tip of my tongue. It couldn't wait to **break free**.

I was saved by Jenny Pinski. That's #1 on my new **Things You Won't Believe In A Million Years** list.

"Tommy and Becca sitting in a tree," Jenny chanted. **"K-i-s-s-i-n-g."**

Becca blushed. Tommy choked on a tater nugget.

"First comes love," Jenny sang. "Then comes marriage."

Nobody shushed her. Jenny might stop singing and start stomping.

"Here they come with a baby carriage," Jenny finished. She laughed loudly, and moved on.

Everyone sitting nearby laughed, too. **Becca's face turned bright red.**

"Tommy and I do not **like-like** each other," Becca protested.

"That's right," **Tommy** agreed. "We're just one-like friends."

"That's not what I heard," **Sylvia** said, stopping next to our table. "*I heard that Tommy and Becca are in love.*"

"Who told you that?" Peter asked. He wasn't tuned in to the **gossip grapevine.**

"I heard it, too," Adam admitted, "from a bunch of different kids."

"Same here," Rusty said.

Becca gasped. "This is only Rusty's second day. If he's heard the rumor, **everybody has**," she said.

Tommy tried to laugh it off. "Everybody can't know something that isn't 𝕋ℝ𝕌𝔼 because there's nothing to know," he told us.

"Oh, yes, there is," Anna said. She stopped next to Sylvia. "I saw you *holding hands* yesterday."

"I fell down and Tommy helped me up," **Becca** said. "That's all."

"Nice guys don't leave girls lying in the **dirt**," Tommy said.

"Puh-lease," **Anna** said. She rolled her eyes and walked away. She sat down at her usual table between Karen and Carly. She whispered in Carly's ear. They both laughed.

Becca turned red. I could tell she was embarrassed.

I was angry. "Anna's a jerk," I said. **"Don't pay any attention to her."**

Monica nodded. "Who cares what Anna says?" she said.

"Everybody," Becca said quietly.

"Not me," Tommy said.

Becca smiled. "Okay," she said. "Everybody but the kids at this table."

That wasn't an exaggeration. At Pine Tree Middle School, Anna's word is law.

Unexplained Law of the Universe: Once a rumor starts — true or false — it's hard to stop.

When Anna Dunlap starts a rumor, it's impossible to stop it.

CHAPTER 7

REJECTION

My inner self was 𝔽𝕌ℝ𝕀𝕆𝕌𝕊 all afternoon. It shouted in my thoughts:

You turned down a study date with Brad!

How could you?

He'll never ask you over to his house again.

Never, never, never!

I can't believe you said no!

I hate it when I won't leave myself alone. **I can't run away!** But I could try to fix the problem.

By study hall, I had an idea. My inner-self stopped yelling and started **cheerleading**.

It's not too late.

Which Claudia are you? Chicken or cool kid?

You can do it!

When the last bell rang, I followed Brad. I only had one chance. It was **do or die, now or never, win or lose**. I stopped him outside the gym.

"I could come over on Friday," I said.

"Friday?" Brad repeated. He shook his head. "I'm busy on Friday."

I went numb.

"I have to go," Brad said. Then he dashed off down the hall.

The world screeched to a halt. I couldn't breathe. I couldn't blink.

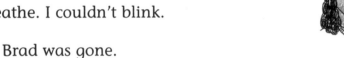

Brad was gone.

The Tell-Tale Signs of a No-chance Romance

1. Brad did not smile.

2. Brad did not say much.

3. Brad couldn't wait to get away.

My maybe-someday daydream of being Brad Turino's girlfriend was **over, finished,** DEAD.

I started breathing before I turned blue. Then I went back to my locker. Becca and Monica were waiting. Becca looked more **miserable** than I felt.

"What's wrong?" I asked.

"Tommy might not be able to go Saturday," Becca said. She took a deep breath. Her lip **quivered**. She was trying not to cry.

"Why not?" I asked.

"He said *he forgot* he had plans with his dad," Becca said quietly. She dabbed her eyes with her sleeve.

"Maybe he did forget," Monica said.

"Or maybe he doesn't want everyone to think the rumor is true," Becca said. She sniffled and added, "Boys hate mushy stuff."

Then it hit me. "Maybe the rumor is **true**," I said.

"Huh?" Becca asked, puzzled.

"Maybe Tommy **really** likes you," I explained.

Becca shook her head. "He made jokes about not liking me," she said.

"Tommy jokes about **everything**," Monica said.

I had another 𝔽𝕃𝔸𝕊ℍ. "You told everyone that you don't like-like Tommy, right?" I pointed out.

Becca nodded.

"But that isn't true," I said. **"You like him a lot."**

"Maybe Tommy likes you a lot, too," Monica said.

"And he's just not ready to admit it," I added.

"You think?" Becca asked. She sniffled again. "You've got to find out, Claudia."

"You want me to ask him?" I asked. **I did not want to ask a boy about love stuff.**

"Yes!" **Becca** exclaimed. "But you can't tell him that I asked you to ask."

"Okay, I'll try," I told her. I wasn't sure Tommy would talk. But helping Becca might take my mind off Brad.

At least one of us would be happy.

CHAPTER 8

DUMPED

Rusty called the next day before breakfast. Grandma answered the phone. I couldn't talk to him. My mouth was full of toothpaste foam.

"Rusty seems like a **nice boy**," Grandma said when I went downstairs. "He's very polite."

"He's okay," I said.

He's not Brad, I thought.

"He called so **early**," Grandma said. She gave me a plate of cinnamon toast. "It must be **important**."

"I'll see him at school," I said.

Brad is avoiding me, I thought.

"What's wrong, Claudia?" **Grandma** asked. She studied my face.

Do I have S-A-D printed on my forehead? I wondered.

"Nothing," I told her.

Grandma knew I was **lying**.

"Can I help?" she asked.

I was so unhappy I broke my **no-love-talk-with-Grandma** rule. "How do you make somebody like you?" I asked.

"Do you mean **like-like**?" Grandma asked.

My cheeks burned, but I nodded. I really wanted to know.

"You can't make anyone LOVE you," Grandma explained. "But that's okay."

No, it's not, I thought.

"Be yourself and **true love** will find you," Grandma told me. She smiled and added, "Honest."

Did that mean Rusty was my true love?

If he was, **why didn't I like-like him back?**

I got to homeroom early. I sat at my desk, minding my own business. Then Jenny decided that my business was her business.

Talking to Grandma about my love life was **weird**.

Talking to Jenny Pinski about it was SCARY.

Tips for Getting Through a Jenny Pinski Q & A

1. When Jenny asks a question, answer.

2. If you lie, Jenny will stomp you.

3. Jenny believes what she wants no matter what you say.

"Where's your boyfriend, Claudia?" Jenny asked. She said the word **boyfriend** like it tasted bad.

"I don't have a boyfriend," I said.

"Yes, you do," Jenny insisted.

"No, I don't," I said. It wasn't smart to disagree with Jenny. **But facts were facts.**

Jenny rolled her eyes. "Everyone knows you like the new kid," she told me.

"Who's everyone?" I asked.

Jenny listed twenty names, including Brad. Everyone thought **Rusty and I were in love.**

Rusty waved and smiled at me when he came into the room.

Brad didn't.

I'm not a quitter. But love isn't a baseball game or a race. It's silly to hang on when there's no hope.

Why Rusty Is A Better Boyfriend Than Brad

1. I don't stammer when I talk to Rusty.

2. Rusty likes me, and Brad doesn't.

3. It's Rusty or no boyfriend at all.

I was dying to know why Rusty called.

Did he just want to talk because he likes me so much?

Was he counting the hours until our movie date?

Would he try to hold my hand?

Rusty was too busy to talk all day. He caught me leaving school, and we walked home together.

It wasn't anything like I imagined.

"My first week at Pine Tree Middle School was fun and easy thanks to you," Rusty said.

I blushed. "I was glad to help," I told him.

"You've been a really great friend," Rusty added.

"I liked getting to know you," I said.

"Me too," Rusty said. He paused. "But . . ."

But . . . means something bad is coming.

It's so awful the person talking doesn't want to say. They have to be pushed.

"But what?" I asked.

"I can't ride to the movies with you and Becca and Tommy tomorrow," Rusty said.

My inner self gasped. *Uh-oh!*

My outer self stayed calm.

"Why not?" I asked.

Rusty blurted out his bad news. "My girlfriend from my old school is coming to visit, and I still like her," he told me. Then he went on, "I want to take Gabrielle to the movies. So I have to break our date."

I couldn't believe it. Rusty was dumping me for his old girlfriend!

"That's okay, Rusty," I said.

"You're not mad?" Rusty asked.

I was FURIOUS.

"No, **I'm not mad**," I lied. "We were just going as friends anyway."

Rusty sighed with relief. "You're the best, Claudia," he said. "See you on Monday."

Rusty turned, and I trudged home alone.

No matter how bad something is, I can usually find things to be glad about. This time I could only think of one.

The Claudia-loves-Rusty rumor would die.

But that didn't make up for the bad thing, which was a thousand times more terrible.

Brad invited me to his house, and I said no.

Now Brad thought I had a boyfriend I didn't have and didn't want in the first place!

CHAPTER 9

LOVES ME, LOVES ME NOT

I expected that talking to Tommy about love would be **weird** or **scary**. But it was almost **impossible**! Of course, I didn't know that when I knocked on his door later that day.

"Hey, Claudia!" Tommy said. He grinned. "What's up?"

"Nothing," I said. "I just came over to say **hello**."

"Okay," Tommy said. He folded his arms and stared at me.

He didn't say anything. Finally, I said, "What?"

"I'm waiting for you to say **hello**," Tommy explained. He kept staring.

I threw up my hands. I forget that Tommy tries to make everything funny. **"Hello!"** I said.

"Okay. Bye!" Tommy said. He started to close the door.

"Wait!" I yelled. I pushed the door open. "Can you talk for **a minute**?"

"Sure," Tommy said. He cleared his throat. Then he looked at his watch and started talking. "I don't know what to talk about so I'll just say whatever pops into my head until **a minute's up** because it doesn't matter what I say as long as the words—"

"Stop!" I yelled.

"That was only **ten seconds**," Tommy said.

I took a deep breath. "I meant I want to talk to you about something," I explained.

"Oh." Tommy came outside. We sat down on the steps. "**I'm all ears**," Tommy said.

I decided to tackle the subject head on. "Do you like-like Becca?" I asked.

Tommy jumped up. "Gotta go!" he said.

It's a good thing I went to talk in person. Tommy couldn't hang up. I yanked him back down.

"This is SERIOUS," I said.

"Why do you want to know?" Tommy asked.

"I can't say," I answered.

"Does Becca like–like me?" Tommy asked quietly.

"I can't say," I said.

"Then I can't say either," Tommy said. He clamped his mouth shut.

I needed an answer. I promised Becca.

"Are you going to the movies tomorrow?" I asked.

"Yep," Tommy answered. "I'd rather see *Alien Hunter* than help Dad clean the garage."

Aha! So Tommy did have plans with his dad! He wasn't trying to get out of the movie date.

"Would you ask any girl to ride with you or just Becca?" I asked.

Tommy didn't pause to think about it. **"Just Becca,"** he told me. "She still wants to go with me, doesn't she?"

"Yes," I said, "but she thinks you're busy with your dad tomorrow."

"**I'll call her tonight,**" Tommy said.

I didn't tell Tommy that Rusty and I weren't going. I wasn't in the mood to explain. **Not to a boy.**

Monica and Becca were in my back yard when I got home. Becca was too 𝒩𝐸𝑅𝒱𝒪𝒰𝒮 to wait in the tree house. She paced back and forth by Mom's garden.

"Did you talk to Tommy?" Becca asked.

I nodded, but I didn't smile. I couldn't resist teasing her a little.

"What did he say?" Becca asked. She closed her eyes and held her breath.

"He made a lot of jokes," I answered. Not a lie.

"That figures," Monica said.

"Then I told him that **Becca really likes him**," I said. It was hard to keep a straight face.

Becca didn't think it was funny. She gasped. "You did not! Did you?" she yelled.

Becca was mortified, and Monica looked shocked. They thought I had broken the **#1 Rule of Middle School Romance For Girls.**

Don't admit you like a boy unless he says he likes you first.

And Never, Ever, Ever tell anyone about boys your friends like.

"No, I didn't," I told Becca.

"Thank goodness," Becca said. She sat down on the garden bench.

"But Tommy asked me **if you like-liked him**," I added. "I just didn't tell him that you did."

"Is that good?" Monica asked. "Does that mean he like-likes Becca?"

"I think so," I said.

"Did he say he liked me?" Becca asked. She crossed her fingers.

"Sort of," I said. "Tommy doesn't have to help his dad clean the garage. So he still wants to go to the movies tomorrow."

Becca smiled. "ＣＯＯＬ!" she said happily.

"And he's going to call you tonight," I explained. "To make sure you still want to go."

The Three Phases of I'm-so-happy-I-can't-stand-it!

1. **Inhale in disbelief.**

2. **Blink and smile as the good news sinks in.**

3. **Jump up, jiggle, and squeal with joy.**

Becca couldn't stop jiggling after I told her what Tommy had said. "This is so great. I can't believe it. Thanks, Claudia," she said, smiling.

"So you guys will have a **real double date** after all!" Monica exclaimed.

"Not exactly," I said. "I'm not going to the movies with Rusty. He's taking Gabrielle."

Becca and Monica stared at me. Their mouths hung open.

"Who's Gabrielle?" they both asked at the same time.

After I filled in the blanks, they were both ANNOYED.

"That is so **unfair**!" Becca said.

Monica's eyes flashed. "I can't believe it. First Rusty acts like your boyfriend. Then he **dumps** you. What a jerk," she said.

"It's okay," I said.

"No, it's not," Becca said angrily. "Anna will blab it all over school, and you'll miss seeing *Alien Hunter*, too."

"You can go with Adam and Peter and me," Monica said.

I shook my head. "That's okay," I said. "I'll see it Sunday, because I have to bring Nick. **I promised**, remember?"

"That's not fun," Monica said.

I sighed. She was right.

Going anywhere with Nick is a test of **babysitter skill and endurance.**

The Nick-At-The-Movies Manual

1. Grab extra napkins. Nick spills soda.

2. Sit behind empty seats. Nick kicks them.

3. Get free-refill popcorn. Nick throws more than he eats.

4. Wear gym shoes. Nick runs up and down the aisles.

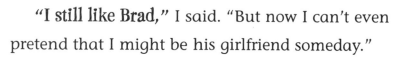

"I can handle Nick," I said. "I'm just glad I'm not going on my first real date with Rusty."

"You are?" Becca asked. She looked confused.

"I still like **Brad,**" I said. "But now I can't even pretend that I might be his girlfriend someday."

Monica scratched her head. "Why can't you?" she asked.

"Brad knows I had a date with Rusty," I explained.

"The date's off," Becca pointed out.

"But everyone thinks I like-liked Rusty," I said. "Brad doesn't know that he's always been **my one and only true love.**"

A tear rolled down my cheek.

I didn't even try to sniffle it back.

CHAPTER 10

BLIND DATE

The next morning, I had the Saturday morning **mopes**. My friends were going out. I was staying home, and hope for Claudia + Brad was gone forever.

I had to go downstairs for breakfast. I didn't want to.

I wasn't sick.

I wasn't in trouble.

And I wasn't hungry.

But Mom and Dad would ask questions if I didn't show up for Grandma's blueberry pancakes.

I gobbled three pancakes and raced back to my room before anyone noticed I had red crying eyes.

I didn't want to **see** anyone.

I didn't want to **talk** to anyone.

And I didn't want to pretend that **everything was fine.**

When the phone rang, I almost didn't answer it. But my brother Jimmy yelled, "Get the phone, Claudia!" I didn't feel like fighting with him.

It was Becca.

"Hi, Becca!" I said. I tried to sound perky. That wasn't easy with a major case of the **deep, dark glooms**. But I didn't want to spoil Becca's happy date day. "What's up?" I asked.

"I've got a huge problem," Becca said.

I could only think of one huge problem that Becca might have today. "Did Tommy cancel your date?" I asked.

"No, but we **almost** called it off," Becca said.

"Why?" I was stunned.

"Because you and Rusty aren't going," Becca said.

"Why is that a problem?" I asked. **"You and Tommy get along great."**

"I know," Becca said, "but we've never been on a date before. What if we say something stupid and ruin it?"

"That's not going to happen," I insisted.

"It won't happen if we have friends along," Becca explained. "Tommy asked someone, and I want you to come."

"I don't know," I asked. "Who did **Tommy** ask?"

"**Some guy** he knows," Becca said.

"I don't want to go on a date," I said.

"It's not a date," Becca said. "It's a movie with friends."

I told Becca I'd call her back.

Then I made two lists.

Why I Shouldn't Go

1. It feels like a blind date even if it's not.

I spent ten minutes trying to think of one more reason not to go. I couldn't.

Why I Should Go

1. I want to see Alien Hunter without Nick.

2. A fake date might look like I dumped Rusty.

3. I could still have a real first date with Brad. Someday.

I called Becca back and said I'd go. Then I spent the next three hours trying to decide what to wear.

Did I want to look smashing? If I couldn't have Brad, I didn't want any boyfriend.

Was it fair to look GREAT and maybe break another guy's heart?

But I didn't want to look like a sloppy loser.

I went for smashing.

I wore my favorite red skirt with a flower print blouse, and put a red clip in my hair.

I was on the front porch when Tommy's minivan pulled up. The side door opened.

"Hi, Claudia!" Becca said. She was sitting in the middle seat with Tommy.

BUTTERFLIES fluttered in my stomach.

I told myself that Tommy's mystery friend was probably nervous too.

I took a deep breath and ran across the lawn to the minivan.

"I hope you don't mind sitting in back," Tommy said.

"I don't mind," I told him. I grabbed the handle to climb inside. I looked at the back seat and froze.

Brad Turino was sitting in the back seat of Tommy's van.

"I hope you're not mad," Brad said.

I struggled to breathe. "Mad? Why would I be mad?" I asked.

Brad took my hand and helped me into the back seat.

He didn't let go when I sat down.

"I didn't want Tommy to tell you that I was your blind date," Brad said. "I was afraid you'd *turn me down* again."

Again?

I stared at Brad. Then it **hit** me. He meant the invitation to his house! It wasn't just a study date. It was an excuse to ask me out!

"This is **my first real date**, Claudia," Brad said. "I wanted it to be with someone I really like."

I was speechless for a second, but I wasn't tongue-tied. **I was thrilled beyond my wildest dreams.**

Brad Turino really liked me!

CHAPTER 11

P.S.

Becca and Tommy stopped caring what other kids thought. They cooked up the blind date so Brad and I could be together, too. The new rumors — **Claudia + Brad** and **Becca + Tommy** — are true!

I wrote a romance for English. In my story, a shy girl wouldn't talk to the boy she liked until they were locked in a classroom. She found out he had a crush on her, too. "Only You" made the school anthology. So did Brad's story, "Madhouse." Anna's rich and famous fashion model story did not. It wasn't ORIGINAL.

Nick's dad took him to see *Alien Hunter* on Saturday. I took him again on Sunday. The cost of breaking a promise to Nick is too high. Never forget: **White glue looks just like shampoo!**

Gabrielle broke up with Rusty because he lives too far away. Now he has a crush on Sylvia. Sylvia like-likes Rusty back.

Brad asked for help with his story because I'm a good writer, but he also wanted to spend time with me.

Wise words to remember: **Be yourself and true love will find you.** I think Grandma is the smartest person in the universe.

About the Author

Diana G. Gallagher lives in Florida with her husband and five dogs, four cats, and a cranky parrot. Her hobbies are gardening, garage sales, and grandchildren. She has been an English equitation instructor, a professional folk musician, and an artist. However, she had aspirations to be a professional writer at the age of twelve. She has written dozens of books for kids and young adults.

About the Illustrator

Brann Garvey lives in Minneapolis, Minnesota with his wife, Keegan, their dog, Lola, and their very fat cat, Iggy. Brann graduated from Iowa State University with a bachelor of fine arts degree. He later attended the Minneapolis College of Art and Design, where he studied illustration. In his free time, Brann enjoys being with his family and friends. He brings his sketchbook everywhere he goes.

Glossary

astonished (uh-STON-ishd)—feeling surprised

casual (KAZH-oo-uhl)—not formal or planned

endurance (en-DUR-uhnss)—how much someone can put up with

flabbergasted (FLAB-ur-gass-tid)—feeling shocked

frantic (FRAN-tik)—wildly excited by nervousness, fear, or worry

furious (FYU-ree-uhss)—very angry

grapevine (GRAYP-vine)—if you hear information through the grapevine, you hear it as a rumor

opportunity (op-ur-TOO-nuh-tee)—a chance to do something

original (uh-RIJ-uh-nuhl)—new, or unusual

quivered (KWIV-urd)—shook

tragic (TRAJ-ik)—disastrous or extremely unfortunate

Discussion Questions

1. Do you think Claudia is too young to have a boyfriend? Or is she too old to just be starting to date? Talk about what you think.

2. Why was Brad upset that Claudia was going out with Rusty? Talk about ways he could have solved the problem.

3. At your school, when two people like each other, what happens?

Writing Prompts

1. Write about your dream first date. Where would you go? What would you do? Who would you be with?

2. Ask your parents, grandparents, or another couple how they met. Write down their story.

3. At the end of this book, Claudia and Brad are going on their first date. What happens next? Write about it.

MORE FUN with Claudia!

POOL PROBLEM

THE COMPLICATED LIFE OF

Claudia
Cristina
Cortez

BY DIANA G. GALLAGHER

REALISTIC FICTION

Claudia Cristina Cortez

Just like every other thirteen-year-old girl, Claudia Cristina Cortez has a complicated life. Whether she's studying for the big Quiz Show, babysitting her neighbor, Nick, avoiding mean Jenny Pinski, planning the seventh-grade dance, or trying desperately to pass the swimming test at camp, Claudia goes through her complicated life with confidence, cleverness, and a serious dash of cool.

David Mortimore Baxter

David is a great kid, but he has one big problem — he can't stop talking. These wildly humorous stories, told by David himself, will show readers just how much trouble a boy and his mouth can get into, whether he's going on a class trip, trying to find a missing neighbor, running a detective agency, or getting lost in the wild. David is amiable, engaging, cool, and smart enough to realize that growing up is the biggest adventure of all.

with David!